For India, Harlem and Remy
From Daddy and Uncle Becksy

LeFT
SH!e
L!ST

Text and Illustrations
copyright © 2016 Left Shoe Lost
All rights reserved

First edition 2017
Printed by Sena Ofset
ISBN - 978-0-9986932-4-8

All designs and illustrations were created digitally and typeset
Felt Tip Roman, Felt Tip Woman, Felt Tip Senior and Forest Puyehue

The paper of this book produced with FSC and PEFC certified paper
acquired from sustainable forest resources. The cover of this book
produced with recycled paper.

The Adventures of CLOUD GIRL

Created by
Dael Oates and Stephen Beck

Since Susie could
remember,

she always wanted
a pet.

But she never could
decide just which pet
to get?

Susie was told,
"Don't just pick
the first one you see"

"Having a pet means loving it,
unconditionally."

So on her favorite hilltop
she looked to the sky.

She hoped that the
clouds could help her
decide.

A turtle can be ridden,
though they move very slow.

A giraffe takes big steps,
but they're hard to pat on
the nose.

Vultures are freaky.

Bats hide
from the sun.

A monkey would be funny,
but the clean up is no fun.

So many to choose,
Susie couldn't decide.

Then she saw
something, right there
in the sky.

A fluffy white cloud!

How about this
little guy?

No fur.
No drool.
No poo-poo on the street.

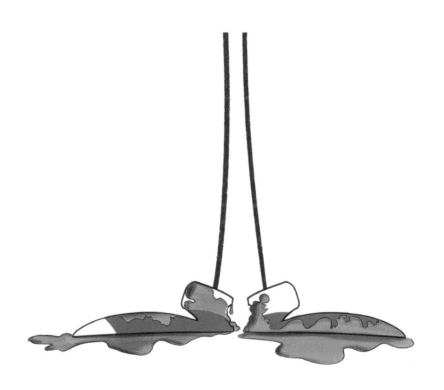

"Mum only needs to worry about
my muddy feet."

Fluffy loves to fetch.

And Fluffy loves to chase.

But when Fluffy barks,

they all run from the place!

There is the occasional
puddle on the floor.

Did you know that a cloud can go under a door?

But the best thing of all is that Fluffy can become...

"ANYTH
IMAGI
UNDER
SUN"

ING I

NE

THE

A teddy,

a whale,

or small like a
mouse.

A GIANT FLUFFASAURUS
AS BIG AS A HOUSE.

A digger.

A robot.

A monster
with big
teeth.

A crazy eight legged
tentacle beast.

Dress-up for tea.

A pirate sailing the sea.

An astronaut in space.

IMAGINATION ALL OVER

TAKES US
THE PLACE

Or what if the water
runs low?

Fluffy could rain
so the gardens can grow.

What if there was a great
burning fire?

No one could stop it, so the
flames just got higher.

Nothing to worry.

Just one quick trip.

Susie clear the building!

FLUFFY
LET IT
RIP!

They'd be heroes,
the town's beloved saviors

Fluffy and Cloud Girl,
Environmental Crusaders!

Susie imagined
all the things
that could be...

Yes, a cloud named Fluffy.

"THAT'S THE PET FOR ME!"

ABOUT THE AUTHORS

Aussie mates, Steve Beck and Dael Oates started their creative journey in Sydney, at the Oscar winning animation studio, Animal Logic (The Matrix, Moulin Rogue!, Happy Feet, The Lego Movie, Lego Batman). It was here Dael and Steve's thirst for storytelling, animation and the power of memorable characters was instilled into them from working along side other talented artists creating world renowned animated films.

From there, Dael became an award winning Commercial and Short film Director and father of three! Steve an award winning Head of Animation, at some of the top studios in the world and beloved uncle!

However Dael and Steve's true passion is to tell their own stories. So they started with this book, The Adventures of Cloud Girl. A story about the power of imagination, told through the adventures of Susie and her shape-shifting pet cloud Fluffy.

Although this book marks the first in a series of Cloud Girl adventures, it also ignites the collaboration on a number of other stories Steve and Dael are developing under their story collective, Left Shoe Lost.

Follow Dael and Steve for updates on
their upcoming stories:
[instagram] @leftshoelost
www.leftshoelost.com